This book belongs to:

....

....

Quarto Knows

Quarto is the authority on a wide range of topics.

Quarto educates, entertains and enriches the lives of our readers—enthusiasts and lovers of hands-on living.

www.quartoknows.com

Author and illustrator: Dubravka Kolanovic
Editor: Ellie Brough
Designer: Victoria Kimonidou

Copyright © QED Publishing 2018
First published in the UK in 2018 by QED Publishing

Part of The Quarto Group
The Old Brewery
6 Blundell Street
London N7 9BH

A catalogue record for this book is available from the British Library.

ISBN 978 1 78493 941 0

Printed in China

MIX
Paper from
responsible sources
FSC® C016973

Kindness is Magic

by Dubravka Kolanovic

It was already late when
Wolf began walking home.

Bump!

He heard a strange noise and saw a
little owl had fallen from a tall tree.

Little Owl ruffled her feathers
and shook her head, but luckily
she did not seem to be hurt.

"Let me help you
get back in the air,"
said Wolf. He picked
Little Owl up and
gently tossed her as
high as he could.

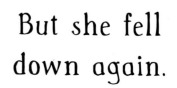

But she fell
down again.

"I don't know
how to fly,"
Little Owl
admitted.

"You can stay with me tonight and I'll help you in the morning," said Wolf.

Wolf stayed up really late that
night. He did lots of research
on flying and owls.

Little Owl did not sleep
either, but owls are
always awake at night.

The next morning, Wolf and
Little Owl went to the top of a
hill. Wolf decided it was the
best place for flying lessons.
Little Owl didn't agree.

"I'm afraid of heights," she said.

"What kind of owl are you? Owls are not supposed to be scared of heights," tutted Wolf.

Wolf thought about what to do.

"Maybe if you had something to hold on to?" he said.

He gave Little Owl a balloon. It was not easy to part with his favourite blue balloon.

Little Owl grasped the balloon but her grip was not tight enough...

And she
fell
down
again.

"What kind of
owl are you?
You're so clumsy!"
said Wolf, upset.

Wolf had another plan. He took a ladder from
his house and brought it to Little Owl's tall tree.

But Little Owl was too
scared to climb alone.
She just clung to Wolf
until they both fell.

"You can't do anything by yourself!"
complained Wolf.

Wolf was tired and was losing his patience.

Little Owl looked at Wolf with her big, sad eyes and sighed. "What kind of owl am I? I'm afraid of heights, clumsy and I can't do anything by myself," she said.

Her words made Wolf blush.
What kind of friend was he?

"I'm sorry I was so mean Little Owl. I am sure you can fly if you really try," said Wolf.

"Just wave your wings like this.
Go on, give it a go."

Wolf encouraged his
friend and Little Owl
tried really, really hard.

She flapped this way and flapped that way, until...

...she found herself flying through the air. It's amazing how **magical** a few kind words can be.

Wolf was very happy for his friend.
She was once again back home, perched
on the branch of the tall tree.

Little Owl was happy too.

At last she could fly.
Little Owl flew back and
gave Wolf a kiss on his nose,
whispering, "Thank you for
being so **kind**."

Next Steps

Discussion and Comprehension

Ask the children the following questions and discuss their answers.

• What did you like most about this story?

• What things were Little Owl afraid of?

• Why did Wolf lose his patience?

• Why was Wolf kind to Little Owl after he'd been cross with her?

Kind Descriptions

Look back through the book with the children and identify the sentences where Wolf was kind. For example: "Let me help you get back in the air." Ask them to think about a time when someone was kind to them. Can they write two sentences, one describing a time when someone was kind to them, and one describing a time when they were kind to someone else? For example: "Mum helped me zip up my coat" and "I shared my treats with Fiona." Ask them to read their sentences out loud.

Kindness Collage

Give the children colour photocopies of all the 'kind' words in the book. For example, 'help', 'gently', 'happy', 'friend', 'gave', 'thank you'. Then give them a piece of blue sugar paper cut into the shape of a large balloon. Ask them to stick the words onto the blue balloon to make a kindness collage. Can the children think of some other kind words to add to their collage?